THIS BOOK BELONGS TO

_____

Mango Allsorts
Brave and helpful; a very good friend indeed.

Bambang
Completely *not*-a-pig; new to the busy city.

Mango's papa

Mostly in his study; welcomes visitors from overseas.

VERY busy— please do not disturb!

Dr. Cynthia Prickle-Posset

A neighbor with a net; doesn't like sweets or children.

George-from-the-Tree-in-the-Park

Keeper of caramels; avoider of baths.

*For my "papa" Tom, who was good at puddings
and stories and kindness and who would have
been happy to share pancakes with a tapir*
P. F.

For Hilary, with love
C. V.

Text copyright © 2015 by Polly Faber
Illustrations copyright © 2015 by Clara Vulliamy

First U.S. edition 2016

Library of Congress Catalog Card Number 2015943770
ISBN 978-0-7636-8226-2

16 17 18 19 20 21 APS 10 9 8 7 6 5 4 3 2 1

Printed in Humen, Dongguan, China

This book was typeset in Veronan.
The illustrations were done in mixed media.

Candlewick Press
99 Dover Street
Somerville, Massachusetts 02144

visit us at www.candlewick.com

Mango
& BAMBANG
The Not-a-Pig

POLLY FABER
illustrated by CLARA VULLIAMY

CANDLEWICK PRESS

Contents

PART ONE

Mango and the Muddle

Mango Allsorts was good at all sorts of things. That was not the same as being good, but she was that, too. Most of the time.

She lived at the very top of a tall building in the middle of a very, *very* busy city.

She lived with her papa, who was also tall and very busy. He spent every day holed up in his study, trying to make books balance. This often took a long time. When, even *after* a long time, the books still wouldn't be balanced, Mango's papa got rather tired. On those days she made him her special buttered noodles.

That was one of the things Mango was good at.

She had a nearly black belt in karate, and she could jump off the highest diving board at the swimming pool without holding her nose, use the Sicilian Defense when playing chess, and wiggle her ears while sucking on a lollipop. She was also learning to play the clarinet. Sometimes the sounds that came out of the bottom were not exactly the sounds Mango had meant when she blew into the top,

but Mango knew
that she just needed
to keep practicing
and soon she would
be good at that, too.

Mango had a lot of time
for practicing; her papa's long hours
balancing meant she had to find her
own things to do. Becoming good at
those things kept her busy. And being
busy was important, living in a very
busy city, full of other busy people being
good at things.

Because otherwise Mango might
have been a little lonely.

It was on a Wednesday that everything changed. It's important to note that it was a Wednesday. A Wednesday can seem a bit of a humpish, nothing-y sort of day, but even humpish sorts of days can hold the unexpected.

In this case the unexpected *was* a hump.

Mango was on her way back from her karate lesson, thinking about how to make her side-thrust kick more effective, when she came to a crosswalk. She was used to having to wait at the curb for all the traffic to stop.

In the very busy city,

drivers were always in a rush, and it

sometimes took them a while to notice

a girl wanting to cross.

But today the traffic was already stopped. In fact it was *very* stopped. Cars were jammed bumper-to-bumper on either side of the road, horns were being honked, and some people had even gotten out of their vehicles and were shouting words they shouldn't have been shouting. It was all a bit of a muddle.

Sorting out a muddle was another thing Mango was good at.

In the middle of the crosswalk a small crowd had gathered around an obstruction. Mango couldn't see exactly what the obstruction was, but with a bit of wriggling and a few polite *Excuse me, please*s, she managed to squeeze through the forest of legs and find out.

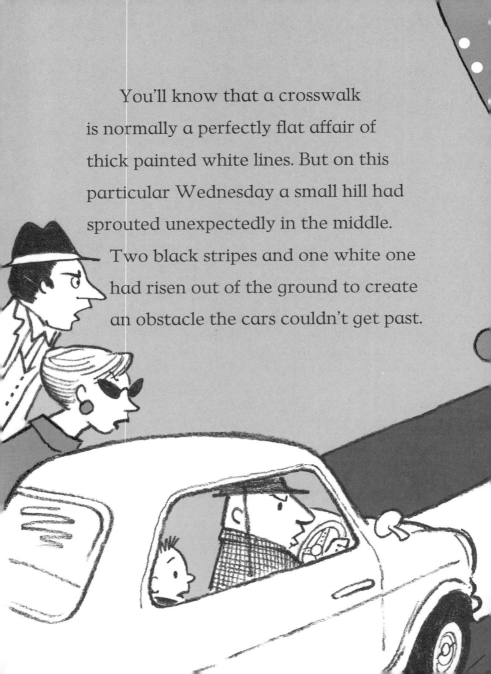

You'll know that a crosswalk is normally a perfectly flat affair of thick painted white lines. But on this particular Wednesday a small hill had sprouted unexpectedly in the middle.

Two black stripes and one white one had risen out of the ground to create an obstacle the cars couldn't get past.

The small crowd was arguing
about where the hill had come
from and what should be done
about it.

"This is a disgrace! I shall be late for
my hair appointment," said a stout man
who didn't seem to have any hair at all.

"It's the underground pipework
gone wrong! I've always said the sewers
in this city are not fit for use. Someone
should inform the authorities," said a
lady in an alarming hat.

"I say we dynamite it! Blow it up, I say. **Kaboom,** I say!" said an overexcited man who kept poking the hump with his umbrella.

Mango noticed the hump was quivering. She knelt down and put a gentle hand on it. It was warm and a little bit hairy. She gave it a comforting scratch and then whispered, "Hello, my name is Mango. Please don't worry. Can I help you?"

Out of one of the black stripes a small, sad eye opened, peered at Mango, then blinked away a tear. The hump shifted a little, and a long black snout unfurled. It sniffled against Mango's open palm in a damp, whiskery sort of way. Very, very softly — so softly, in fact, that nobody but Mango could hear it — the hump whispered a warning:

"Tiger!"

Then the eye shut, the snout tucked in, and the hump curled into a tight mound once more.

The quivering turned into violent shaking.

"*Eek!* It's alive! It's got NOSTRILS! It's a mutant sewer pig! They're surging up from the pipes! They'll come out of our toilets and eat us in our beds at night!" shrieked the alarming-hat lady.

"I read about mutant pigs in the paper, I'm sure of it," said the bald man, nodding in a definite way. "Shocking."

"Send in the air force! Mobilize the army! Press the big red button that fires the big fat bomb!" The overexcited man was jumping from foot to foot and jabbing his umbrella in the air.

Mango made herself tall and folded her arms. She looked at them all. She spoke in her best voice for calming people who are being silly. She was good at that, too.

"You are all being ridiculous. This is *not* a **pig,** or a danger. Anyone sensible can see this is clearly a **tapir** from the jungles of Malaysia. He must have taken a wrong turn somewhere along the way. I expect one tree looks much like another if you wander too far."

"A tapir? Never heard of it. Don't believe in it," said the bald man. Mango gave him a pitying look. The crowd began to go back to their vehicles. She knelt down and talked to the tapir once more.

"A tiger sounds very alarming. But I promise there isn't one now. Won't you uncurl and cross the road with me? I'm going home to make banana pancakes for my papa. We'd love for you to join us."

Slowly, under Mango's encouraging strokes, the shaking first settled, then stopped . . . and the hump changed shape. From out of the crosswalk the black-and-white lines resolved themselves into a really rather marvelous black-and-white creature.

Have you ever met a tapir? You need to keep a careful watch for them when out and about; they are nervous animals, inclined to jumpiness, and tend to hide when scared. It takes a very special person to be trusted by a tapir.

"Banana pancakes?" said the tapir, in a hopeful whisper. He didn't seem quite ready to move.

"With syrup and whipped cream, too, if you like," said Mango gently. She sensed this was a tapir who should not be hurried.

HONK, HONK!

BEEP, BEEP!

The people in the traffic jam were less patient. A lot of rather noisy engine revving was beginning to happen. There were shouts of "Oh, come *on*!" and "Move it along, now!" too.

"I've never had syrup or whipped cream *or* a pancake before," said the tapir, his voice getting less whispery. "But I do like bananas very much indeed."

"Papa and I would be delighted to introduce you to all those things and more," said Mango. "Were you planning a long visit to the city? We have plenty of room for you to stay. I'm so sorry—I don't know your name." She glanced at the ever-growing traffic jam.

TING-A-LING-A-LING!

The overexcited man was now
talking overexcitedly to a policeman
on a motorcycle, who was writing in a
notebook. A line of pedicabs had joined
the line, and their bells were ringing
impatiently. So was the louder bell of
the halted Express City Trolley.

"My name is Bambang," said the tapir.
"And your offer sounds very kind. I *am*
a little tired. I ran a great distance and
swam, and there was a boat, I think,
although I am not perfectly sure, but
certainly more running. And there was a
tiger . . . a hungry tiger, you see . . ." As he
spoke, the tapir started to look anxious
again, as if he might curl straight back
into a ball.

Mango, aware of a helicopter now starting to circle overhead, was quick to reassure him. "There are no tigers in the city, Bambang. Apart from at the zoo, perhaps, but they're safely locked up and kept very well fed, I should think."

Suddenly the policeman bellowed

through a megaphone:

"ALL GIRLS AND POSSIBLE MUTANT PIGS MUST CLEAR THE ROADWAY! REPEAT — ROADWAY MUST BE CLEARED OF ALL PIGS IMMEDIATELY, OR FORCIBLE REMOVAL WILL BE EFFECTED."

He started to direct the cars

to one side, apparently making space

for something else to come through.

"No tigers at all?" The tapir peered up at Mango.

"None."

"Then I would very much like to try a pancake and maybe stay a *little* while. If you're sure it would be no trouble?" And with that, to Mango's relief, Bambang started to cross the road.

Her relief was short-lived.

They hadn't moved more than a couple of steps before there was an unfortunate setback.

The drivers, seeing the tapir start to move, all put their feet on their gas pedals at once, creating a sudden, definitely *tiger*-ish roar. This was enough to startle Bambang.

At the same time, he spotted something on the other side of the road that sent him curling up tight again.

"*Tiger!*" he shouted. The crosswalk, or tapir not-crossing, as it might more accurately have been called, was blocked once more.

Mango felt alarmed. She could see the policeman had been clearing cars to make way for a giant scooping digger. That giant scooping digger was now maneuvering into position and lowering its huge scoop. There seemed little doubt that what it was intending to scoop was Bambang.

Mango looked across the road. She remembered that tapirs are known to have rather poor eyesight. She suddenly realized what had frightened Bambang.

"Well, this is quite a muddle," Mango said to herself.

She went up to the policeman. "Could I possibly borrow your megaphone for a moment?" she asked.

With her hand out, she stood firmly in front of the digger. It juddered to a surprised stop.

Mango climbed on top of its scoop and addressed the waiting traffic.

"THERE IS A TAPIR HERE. HE WILL CROSS THE ROAD BUT HE IS FEELING A BIT NERVOUS. HE HAS NEVER BEEN IN A BUSY CITY BEFORE, YOU SEE. I THINK IT WOULD BE VERY HELPFUL IF YOU COULD ALL TURN OFF YOUR ENGINES FOR A MOMENT AND STOP SHOUTING AND BEEPING AND RINGING YOUR BELLS, AND THEN I CAN TALK TO HIM CALMLY AND WE WILL BE ON OUR WAY FOR BANANA PANCAKES VERY SHORTLY."

Mango started to hand back the megaphone, but then she put it to her lips again. "THANK YOU," she added.

There was a pause and then, one by one, the shouting people, the cars, the pedicabs, the trolley, and the digger fell silent. The helicopter moved discreetly away.

Mango leaned down to the Bambang-shaped hump and talked soothingly into where she hoped his ear might be.

"Bambang, dear Bambang, there really, truly, honestly is no tiger. Did you perhaps see that tabby cat on the wall over there and *think* it was a tiger? I can see that it might be very easy to confuse a close-up cat with a faraway tiger. If you'll only uncurl, I can show you the difference. And then you can come home and meet Papa and eat bananas and try pancakes and stay." She tickled his white stripe.

Inside his ball, Bambang thought and thought some more. On the one foot there was the possibility of a tiger, on another was the promise of pancakes, and on a third there was Mango. He had always been very fond of mangoes. He didn't even need to use his fourth foot. He brought his head out again and crossed bravely to the sidewalk.

Walking home with her new friend, Mango found herself feeling not perfectly certain what having a tapir come to stay might involve.

And that was a very exciting feeling indeed.

• PART TWO •

Bambang's Pool

Bambang wriggled and pushed his snout through the small gap at the bottom of the window. The rain pitter-pattered against his nose. By stretching out his tongue as far as it would go, he could catch the drops as they fell. He gave a little sigh.

He'd been in the city a month.
A month full of sights undreamed of
when he'd run and run and swum and
hidden and run some more away from
the jungle. Bambang still hid, sometimes
several times a day, from possible tigers,
but he'd not met a single *real* one in all
that time. Instead he had met automatic
doors and ice cream and trolleys and
bubbles in fizzy lemonade and kites and
turnstiles and so many
other wonderful things.
Best of all, he'd
met them with
wonderful
Mango.

There was only one thing he missed.

Mango looked up from her chess-board at the sigh. She had been trying out a new pawn opening.

"Oh, Bambang! What's the matter? Are you missing your pond?"

It couldn't be hidden. Tapirs love water. In his patch of jungle Bambang had lived near a cool pool of weeds and mud where he'd wallowed and rolled his cares away. On days like this, when the rain came down, the smell brought back memories. It was the only thing he missed, but he *did* miss it.

"Do you want me to run you a bath again?" asked Mango.

Bambang shook his head. He'd tried the bathtub, but it wasn't the same. The problem was that not all of him fit in it at once. Either he had to drape his front legs over the edge or hang his bottom out the back. It was undignified.

"I know!" said Mango, getting up from her chessboard. "We'll go swimming. Properly. At the public pool."

Bambang's ears and snout both pricked up at that suggestion. He liked the idea.

What is your nearest public pool like? Does it have exciting things like wave machines and curly slides and bubbly bits? Or is it just a plain rectangle?

The very busy city where Mango lived had the rectangle sort. The very busy people didn't have time for curly slides.

There were two rectangles there. A small deep one, with diving boards beside it for practicing jumping and diving, and a long thin one, divided into lanes for going back and forth. Bambang looked at the diving boards with a keen interest. There was nothing like *them* in the jungle. He wanted to try one right away.

Mango said it might be better to *start* with the back-and-forth pool.

It was divided into three lanes, marked with strict signs that read **SLOW**, **MEDIUM**, and **FAST**. Bambang and Mango looked at each other, not sure which one they should choose. The other people in the pool were no help.

In the **FAST** lane a man with a serious mustache was flapping his arms and kicking his legs in an energetic manner, but not moving anywhere at all.

The **SLOW** lane had a line of very old ladies, all bobbing and gliding like clockwork through the water.

It seemed rather full.

They settled for **MEDIUM**.

Bambang was just about to get in when a fierce man in a tank top and shorts blew his whistle and pointed.

"The pig needs a swim cap: no swim cap, no swim," he said.

Mango rolled her eyes. "I'm so sorry, Bambang. A **pig** indeed! Come out of your ball; the lifeguard's *not* a tiger — he's just a big silly. You can borrow my spare swim cap."

When he'd unrolled himself,
Bambang thought he'd never seen
anything as magnificent as Mango's
spare swim cap. It was his first hat.
He liked it very much indeed.

They got in the water and began
to swim.

At first Bambang was happy.
It was lovely to have the whole
of his body in the water
once more,

to dive and roll
and duck under and blow bubbles
with his nose.

But it wasn't like his jungle pool. The water smelled wrong, and there was no sticky mud to squish his toes into or weeds to play hide-and-seek with the fish in.

And swimming back and forth in a rectangle isn't very exciting.

Bambang started swimming faster and faster. He raced from one end of the pool to the other at a very not-**MEDIUM** speed. He made a

wave behind him, which spread out
to the other corners of the pool. The
old ladies found themselves bobbing
in increasingly choppy waters. The
flapping man spluttered as water
swept over his mustache.

Then Bambang went zigzagging
under the water, using his snout
as a snorkel.

He swam right underneath the old ladies. He waved his snout cheerily at them as he surfaced on the other side. They waved back. The man in the tank top blew his whistle again.

"Keep in your lane, pig," he said.

But Bambang had had enough of lanes. He got out of the pool and shook himself dry. He looked again at the diving boards.

"Let's try that now. Can we? Can we *please,* Mango?"

"Are you sure you'll like it, Bambang?" Mango was a little doubtful. Bambang nodded. "Then of course we can."

It was a
very,
very
long
climb
to the highest
diving board.
Mango led the
way. Bambang
started to
feel less sure
about whether
he'd like it as he
went up each
rung of the
ladder.

At the very
top Mango stood
poised and tall
on the end of
the board, then
stepped off,
her toes neatly
pointed. She
landed in the pool
with a small *plop,*
sending out rings
of perfectly even
ripples.

Bambang was left on his own.
He peered over the edge, nervously.
In the distance Mango smiled up at
him. The water seemed a worryingly
long way away. He decided the best
approach would be to shut his eyes
and just run for it.

Bambang launched himself off
at considerable speed.

For a moment he was airborne and
free — the world's first flying tapir — his
ears and snout blowing upward. Then
he made the mistake of opening his eyes.
Terror gripped him. Bambang shrieked
and bundled into a tight, tight ball as he
hurtled toward the water.

Water went *everywhere*.

Well, almost everywhere; not much was left in the pool.

"Pig, *out!*" shouted the man in the now-dripping-wet tank top. He couldn't even blow his whistle. It was too full of pool water.

Bambang got *out*. He was mortified. He didn't even look for Mango. He didn't hear her shout, "Oh, Bambang, I'm so sorry! I shouldn't have left you up there. Wait! Bambang—*come back!*" He just ran.

Tapirs can run fast. They learn to when they're very small or else they get eaten.

Mango, who had never had to worry about being eaten, and who had to grab towels and clothes and shoes and all the other things tapirs are lucky enough to do without, could not keep up with Bambang.

In fact Mango Allsorts, hurrying out of the public pool, found she had *lost* a tapir. And though she *was* good at all sorts of things, she found she was not good at having lost a tapir *at all*.

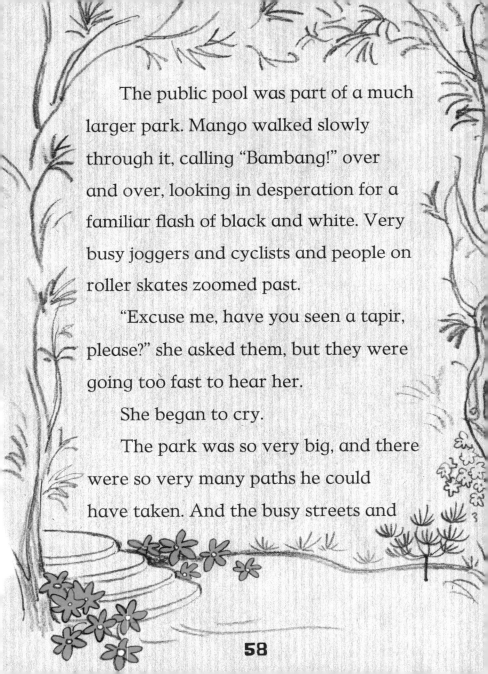

The public pool was part of a much larger park. Mango walked slowly through it, calling "Bambang!" over and over, looking in desperation for a familiar flash of black and white. Very busy joggers and cyclists and people on roller skates zoomed past.

"Excuse me, have you seen a tapir, please?" she asked them, but they were going too fast to hear her.

She began to cry.

The park was so very big, and there were so very many paths he could have taken. And the busy streets and

tall buildings beyond the park were a
bewildering maze. Mango knew that if
Bambang had gone that far she would
never find him.

　　She sat down on a bench. She felt
hopeless. Her crying became the bigger,
wetter, hiccupy, messy sort.

A large gold-wrapped caramel dropped from the sky into her lap. Mango stopped hiccuping and looked up, startled. A face was grinning down at her from the branches of a tree above.

"It's a good one. You look like you need it. Bad day?" the face said.

It was quite a grubby face, but friendly. It belonged to a boy.

Mango wiped her nose and eyes. After all, feeling hopeless would not find Bambang. She unwrapped the caramel and popped it in her mouth.

"I didn't know you were there. I've lost my friend," she said.

"I'm often up here. Nobody knowing is sort of the point. Everything's better in a tree. Fewer people trying to clean you up with wet washcloths and make you put on sport coats to stand on balconies and wave at boring parades," said the boy with feeling. "Who's your friend? How did you lose him?"

"He's black and white and people think he looks like a pig, which is stupid of them. He got scared at the public pool," explained Mango. "He often gets scared."

The boy looked thoughtful. "He's not a *tapir,* is he? A tapir in a . . . swim cap?"

"Yes!" said Mango. "Oh, *yes!* Have you seen him? Please, have you seen him?"

"Want to take a look?" The boy stuck a slightly sticky hand through the leaves. Mango grabbed it and quickly climbed up.

"I'm George. Welcome to my tree," said the boy when she reached his branch. It was a bit of a squeeze.

George seemed to have more than
the normal amount of knobby elbow
and knee. Also, quite a lot of stuff was
stored in his tree. He shuffled along to
make space. "Is that your friend?"

Mango looked where George was
pointing. Up high she had a perfect
view over the tops of flowerbeds and
bushes. Her heart lifted. For there, not
too far away, was Bambang.

He was sliding down the tail of a
golden horse, part of a park monument
to the first man who had ever been busy
in the very busy city. It was a statue in
the middle of a pool full of ornamental
fish and water lilies, surrounded by jets
of splashing
water.

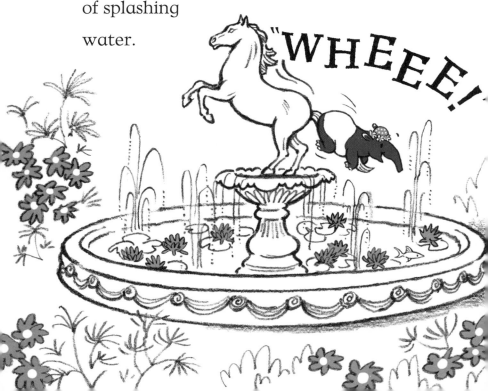

"WHEEE!"

"Bambang!" she said. "Oh, that *is* my friend! Everything really *is* better in a tree! Thank you, George. I must go to him." She started to get down.

"That's OK," said George. "Can I come, too? I don't know many tapirs. Does he like caramels?"

"I don't know if he's ever had one, but I'm *sure* he'd like to try. Just don't mention tigers," said Mango. "Or blow a whistle," she added.

Bambang ducked under a water lily at the sound of Mango's and George's footsteps. But he popped out again as soon as he saw who it was.

"Where have you been?" He blew water at Mango, happily. "Look! I've found a much better pool. It has fish to play with, it's squishy on the bottom, and the water stays in the pool where it's supposed to be. It smells right." He didn't realize he'd been found. He'd completely forgotten about running away. He hadn't known he'd been lost in the first place.

If Mango had been a different sort of girl, she might have reminded him. She might have gotten cross. She might have told Bambang off for the worry he'd caused her.

Luckily, Mango was not that sort of girl.

So instead she introduced George. And George introduced caramels. And *didn't* mention tigers or whistles. And Bambang found he *did* like caramels. And they talked about city trees and jungle trees. And about city pools and jungle pools. And those who had shoes and socks took them off and waded with those who didn't.

And everyone felt very pleased with everyone else.

And Bambang didn't miss anything anymore.

• PART THREE •

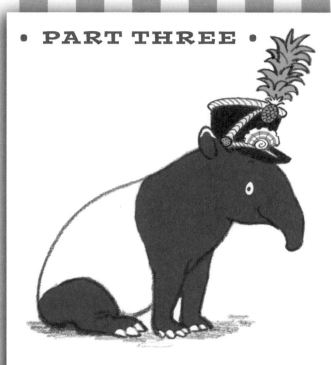

Bambang
Puts On a
Hat

With a new pool, a new friend and, above all, with Mango, Bambang was truly happy. Mango was happy, too. But she was also a little wary. She knew that although there were no tigers in the very busy city, there were other dangers to a tapir of increasing curiosity. And some dangers were closer to home than Mango quite liked to think. She made Bambang promise never to go out without her.

So while Mango was at school, Bambang stayed at home. He was allowed anywhere in the apartment except the study, where Papa worked all day and sometimes all night on his books. There was a big **DO NOT DISTURB** sign up. Bambang was careful to be quiet near the door. But when Mango's papa was lost in his balancing, he seemed to forget about everything else. Including tapirs in his apartment.

EVEN MORE BUSY —
please do not disturb!

Bambang passed most of his time sleeping or stretching or looking out the window, but he did other things, too.

Trying on hats, for example. After the success of the swim cap, Mango and her papa had lent him a small collection. Bambang found that each of the hats made him feel a little bit different.

He had a Being-Silly Hat,

a Thoughtful Hat,

a Party Hat,

and a Comforting Hat.

He also had a Very
Brave Hat. And one
particularly slow

waiting day, Bambang put it on.
It wasn't that he *forgot* his promise to
Mango; he just thought he'd take a tiny
peek out the front door. As long as he
stayed in the apartment building he
wasn't really going out . . .
was he?

Two of Bambang's favorite wonders-that-weren't-in-the-jungle were the stairs and the elevator in the apartment building. When he and Mango went out together, he'd race down all the stairs as quickly as he could and see if he could beat Mango in the elevator. (Mango always made sure he won.)

Coming back up again, they would
take the elevator together. Bambang
would stretch and press the top button
with his snout. He enjoyed the strange
jump in his tummy as they were
whooshed up to the top floor.

But he had never been out there on
his own before.

The building was very quiet during the daytime. Everyone was out being busy. Bambang was pleased to have the place to himself. He was *not* very quiet.

But not *everyone* was out.

In the apartment on the floor below Mango's, Dr. Cynthia Prickle-Posset had just returned from a long trip overseas.

If Mango— currently pouring the contents of one test tube into another at school—had known this, she would have worried.

If she'd known about Bambang putting on his Very Brave Hat, too, she would have worried even more.

For Mango knew Cynthia Prickle-Posset was not a tiger. She was *much* worse than that.

Bambang galloped down the
stairs and took the elevator back up
to Mango's floor three times. Then he
decided to experiment.

First he tried bumping down some
of the stairs.

BA-DOOM!

BA-DOOM!

BA-DOOM!

went Bambang's bottom. It was fun, but
not very comfortable.

Next he tried sliding down them
back feet first.

SHHLOMF-A!

SHHLOMF-A!

SHHLOMF-A!

went Bambang's tummy. It was
interesting, but a bit shaky-uppy.

Finally he climbed onto the banister and went hurtling down snout first at top speed.

"AIEEEAIEEAIEEEE!"

went Bambang.

He landed in a heap at the bottom.

That, Bambang decided, was rather *too* exciting.

Upstairs, Cynthia Prickle-Posset had been listening intently. She started to unpack her traveling trunk. There was equipment in there that she would need.

Feeling slightly out of breath, Bambang began a slower exploration of the other floors in the building. As he got in the elevator this time, he pressed each button in turn and had a careful look as the doors opened on each level. There wasn't that much to see. Most lobbies had bare walls and a front door, much like Mango's.

One had a poster up advertising dance classes. Bambang was impressed. He looked at what the couple were doing with their feet and tried to copy them. He was *not* successful. He decided he would ask Mango about taking the classes.

The next floor had a fancy table outside the door, with an enormous vase of flowers on it. Bambang had a drink of water from the vase. All the going down stairs and dancing had made him quite thirsty. He made a *small* mess. He hoped nobody would mind.

This time, as he got back into the elevator, a strange thing happened. The doors closed and the elevator began rising without him pressing any buttons at all. Bambang felt nervous. A little of his bravery slipped away. He shut his eyes and hoped the elevator was just taking him home.

But it stopped one floor short of home. When Bambang opened his eyes, he saw the lobby of Cynthia Prickle-Posset's apartment. He saw Cynthia Prickle-Posset herself waiting for him, her finger on the elevator's call button. And he knew right away that he'd picked the wrong day to try on hats.

Home at last, Mango opened the front door of her apartment. "Bambang," she called, "I made double-chocolate brownies for us at school. Would you like some?"

There was no reply. No warm tapir rushed into her arms. No tapir tongue began licking her face all over. The apartment was silent.

Mango took a brownie in to Papa. His books were having a particularly lopsided day. He had no idea that Bambang had gone.

Then, through the floor, they both heard a series of muffled thumps, bangs, shouts, and awful shrieks coming from the apartment below. Now Mango was worried; dreadfully worried. She smoothed down her hair and her skirt, picked up her plate of brownies, and prepared to pay a visit to her neighbor.

Do you collect anything? Fruit stickers or especially smooth pebbles or pictures of cats, perhaps? Cynthia Prickle-Posset was a collector. She called herself a Collector of the Unusual. She traveled all around the world looking for Unusual Things. Her collection filled her apartment and spilled out into her lobby.

Mango and her brownies had to squeeze through a jumble of the Unusual to find Cynthia Prickle-Posset's front door. Among other things, Mango saw an enormous jar of pickled puffer fish, a crate of assorted large bones, part of a rhino, and a mysterious box labeled **MUSTACHES OF FAMOUS MURDERERS.** She rang the bell, trying not to look too closely.

Cynthia Prickle-Posset opened the door a crack. She often looked red in the face, but she was quite scarlet today. She seemed a little out of breath, too.

"Good afternoon, Dr. Prickle-Posset. I see you've returned from your latest trip. I do hope it was a successful one. I thought you might like some brownies? I made them myself." Mango was *always* polite.

"Go away, little girl. I am busy and I don't *like* sweets." Cynthia Prickle-Posset was less polite. There were squeals and banging and crashing noises behind her.

CRASH! "EEK!" "SQUEAL!"

Cynthia Prickle-Posset looked around and started to close the door. Mango stuck out her foot to stop her.

"Only I've lost my friend Bambang and I wondered if you might have seen him. He's a tapir. Visiting from Malaysia," Mango added helpfully.

Cynthia Prickle-Posset turned a shade redder still. "I have *no* knowledge of Malaysian visitors. Or"—she coughed—"*tapirs.* Remove your foot and return to your *dolls* or whatever little girls like you play with. I have things to *do* with my *Collection.*"

The banging noises behind her got even louder. Cynthia Prickle-Posset began to push at the door. Mango stood her ground.

"It's quite a noisy Collection, isn't it? Almost like something is trying to escape. Almost like something *doesn't want* to be Collected." She spoke in a louder voice.

"Mango! Is that you? Oh, help! Help me, *please*!" Bambang's voice came from inside.

"Remove your foot *now*, or I shall *feed* it to my giant carnivorous plant," said Cynthia Prickle-Posset, sharply.

Mango couldn't be polite any longer.

Bambang needed her. She brought her other foot up in a perfectly positioned karate kick.

The door jolted open, allowing her to step past a caught-off-guard Cynthia Prickle-Posset and inside. Mango put down the plate of brownies on a handy table made from the shell of a giant tortoise and ran to Bambang.

Poor Bambang. All of him was wrapped in an enormous net, and half of him was squeezed into a glass case as well. Cynthia Prickle-Posset had obviously not been fully prepared for the sudden capture and display of a tapir. The case had contained a stuffed warthog, which had been thrown on the floor to make room for Bambang.

Tapirs are rather bigger than warthogs. And live tapirs, not in the mood to be Collected, are even more difficult to fit in cases. Mango felt quite

proud of Bambang. Once upon a time,
he would have just curled into a ball.
Now, it was clear, he could make quite
a big mess.

"Oh, Mango, I put on a Very-*too*-Brave Hat and went sliding and at first it was fun and then it wasn't and then I went exploring and at first *that* was fun and then it wasn't and you told me not to and I shouldn't have and now I've been Collected and I don't like it *at all*!" wailed Bambang.

"I should think not," said Mango. "Now we're going to un-Collect you and take you home." She pulled Bambang out of the case and started to unwrap the net.

"What do you think you're *doing*? *Barging* into private property! Hands off that *exhibit*. It is *not* for touching. That's my *unusual wild beast*. *That tapir is mine.*" Cynthia Prickle-Posset was positively purple now. She was also brandishing a *particularly* bristly broom at Mango.

Mango wished she were wearing a Very Brave Hat of her own. She felt horribly wobbly inside. She also knew she mustn't show the wobbliness. It wasn't so different from a tricky game of chess.

"We will be very pleased to leave,
Dr. Prickle-Posset, and plan to do so
as soon as this net is off. Bambang
is not available to be Collected, you
see." Mango gave a final tug and freed
Bambang. "He is not *yours,* and he is not
mine either. He is not *anybody's.* He is a
guest in our city. Wild beasts, after all,
do not wear hats. And exhibits do not
eat double-chocolate brownies . . . Leave
some for our neighbor, Bambang!"

Bambang looked up,
a little shamefacedly, from the now
rather emptier plate.

"I'm very sorry," he whispered. "I
was unusually hungry. But usual in all
other ways!" he added hastily, in case he
was about to be Collected again.

Mango took a deep breath and
walked straight past Cynthia Prickle-
Posset and out the door, Bambang
trotting at her side.

"This is not the *end* of this *matter*," said Cynthia Prickle-Posset as they left. "Tapirs are *not* guests, whatever you may say. They belong in *zoos* or in the hands of *adult* experts. You *will* be hearing from me again. *I will have that creature*."

But she set down her broom.

Safe in the elevator, for the time being, at least, Mango and Bambang hugged each other very, very tightly.

"Oh, Mango," said Bambang finally,

"I promise I shall never, *ever* wear that hat again."

"Oh, Bambang," said Mango. "You shall wear whatever hat you choose. Always. But maybe not for the rest of this afternoon? Or at least not until after supper."

• PART FOUR •

The Song
of the
Tapir

Bambang did a lot more curling into a ball again in the days after meeting Cynthia Prickle-Posset. And despite Mango's gentle encouragement he did rather less trying on of hats, too. Mango, although still somewhat wobbly in her own tummy about the whole affair, said he wasn't to worry, since their neighbor never stayed for long.

Mango was very relieved to be

proved right about this. A week later Bambang and Mango were returning with important supplies from the corner store when they saw Cynthia Prickle-Posset leaving the building.

She was dressed in her full Collector's outfit and was loading a taxi with lots of equipment, including a suit of armor, a lasso, and a cage with iron bars. She was obviously planning to hunt out some *particularly* Unusual Things. Bambang shuddered. He hoped they would take a very long time to find.

Mango and Bambang hid, not terribly successfully, behind a lamppost.

They could feel the eyes of Cynthia Prickle-Posset watching them. She gave a loud *harrumph*, like an angry elephant. But then they heard the trunk being shut and the taxi driving away.

Mango opened some of their important supplies to celebrate.

Even with Cynthia Prickle-Posset gone, Bambang still felt troubled. Mango had given him so much. He wished he could give her something in return.

And then he got his chance.

One day Mango's footsteps as she came home from school were slower and heavier than usual, a change only a finely tuned tapir's ear could hear. Bambang knew Mango needed a *particularly* loving head rub. She pulled his ears in a distracted way.

"Oh, phooey, Bambang. Phooey and pooh. It's the Big City Concert tomorrow, and I just can't get my notes right. Papa's coming, and I so want to be good. I've been practicing and practicing my clarinet, but the more I practice, the worse I sound. I'm just *not* any good."

Bambang thought Mango was wonderful. He was her biggest fan. He *knew* she was good at all sorts of things — making tapirs happy and safe, for instance. That was the best thing of all to be good at.

But he also knew that she was right about her clarinet playing. It *wasn't* good.

He stroked her face gently with his snout.

"Perhaps you don't have to play? Your papa will understand," he suggested.

Mango was stern. "Now, Bambang. We've talked about this before. If one gives up on things just because they're hard at first, one never gets good at anything. Look at how good you've gotten at being brave about tigers and Collectors. That's because you've practiced. I'll just have to practice all night." She looked determined. And a little sad.

Bambang nodded. Mango's attitude was inspiring. He just wasn't sure more practicing was the answer this time. He had a thought: perhaps he *could* be of use?

"Sometimes," he said, gently, "music needs to be felt as well as played. What's the piece that you're playing tomorrow and how do you feel when you're playing it?"

"It's called 'City Nights' and I feel worried and cross," said Mango immediately.

"Then that's what we need to work on," said Bambang. His thought was clearer now. "And I know just how to help."

It was very nearly midnight.
Mango was woken by a tapir
blowing softly in her ear.

She put on her slippers, picked
up her clarinet case, and followed
Bambang out of the apartment. It was
time for an adventure.

Have you ever been out somewhere
you normally only go in the daytime
very late at night? It feels quite, *quite*
different and new. Standing in the
darkness in her pajamas, Mango
bounced on her toes and clapped
her hands.

"Oh, this is lovely! Where shall we
go first?"

The streetlights made glowing
pools. The dark shadows beyond
their reach seemed extra black. But
Bambang, even without a brave-
making hat on, was not a bit scared of
the dark. He knew his nose and ears
would not let him down. He caught an
interesting scent on the warm night

breeze and set off to follow it. Mango kept her hand on his shoulder. It was her turn to need a little reassuring.

They passed open doorways with the sounds of music and laughter spilling out. Mango looked in curiously, but Bambang didn't stop. The very busy city was less busy at night. People passing them in the street walked more slowly, arm in arm, chatting to each other in low voices. The vehicles were different and slower, too. Mango felt Bambang give a nervous shiver as the whirring brushes of a street-cleaning truck passed by. She gave him a squeeze. "No tigers. No Collectors, either," she said.

They reached the main square, and here it *was* busy. A collection of small wooden stalls had been set up, all lit with colorful paper lanterns. They were selling many different delicious things to eat — the smells that had beckoned to Bambang. Here, too, there was music. A group of musicians with stringed instruments was playing, and people were dancing. Mango bought a cone of candied nuts, and a paper bag of fresh pineapple fritters. They shared them as they walked on.

"This is a wonderful treat, Bambang, but I still don't understand how it's going to help me play my clarinet tomorrow," said Mango.

"Just a little bit farther."

Only when they reached a wide stone bridge did Bambang stop.

Running through the heart of the very busy city was a river. By day, its brown waters carried ships full of cargo and people in and out of the town. By night, it was calmer. Mango and Bambang hung over the edge. They watched the reflection of the round yellow moon swirl and shimmer in the current.

Farther down the river, the end of
the city and the beginning of the ocean
were just in sight. Beyond that, a *long*
way beyond that, lay Bambang's
jungle. Everything was still
and quiet.

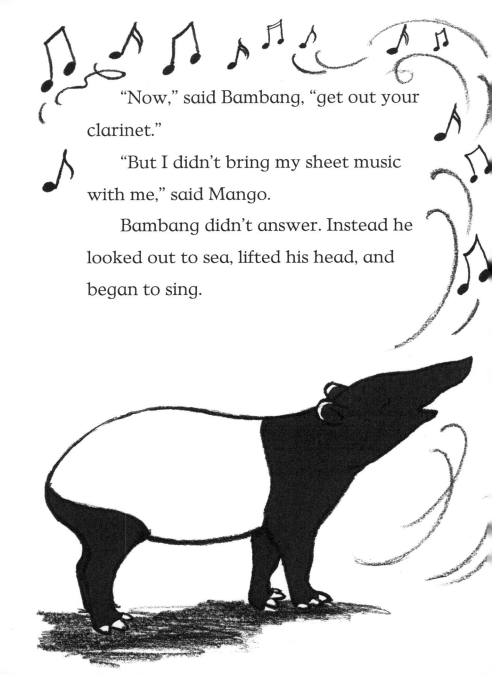

"Now," said Bambang, "get out your clarinet."

"But I didn't bring my sheet music with me," said Mango.

Bambang didn't answer. Instead he looked out to sea, lifted his head, and began to sing.

All baby tapirs learn the Song of the Tapir before they can talk. It may be the oldest song of all, passed down unchanged from mother to calf for hundreds and hundreds of years. Its simple whistled notes speak of jungles and tigers and love and loss and the niceness of bananas as nothing else can.

Very few people have ever been allowed to hear it. Now Mango was one of them.

She listened.

She felt.

She understood.

She picked up her clarinet and began to play.

Together, they made music.
They sent up their song — over the city,
down the river, out to the sea and the
beyond-the-sea. It was good.

The next day, in the concert hall, the audience was packed in. Bambang sat toward the back next to Mango's papa. He was finding it hard to remember he could be brave in a crowd and was trying not to curl into a ball. There had been some confusion at the door about the correct ticket price for a tapir. Nobody quite seemed to know, files had been checked, and he'd heard the *pig* word muttered.

A lady with a bustling, almost Collector-ish air, dressed in an unfortunate dress of orange stripes, tried to squeeze past him to get to her seat. She made loud tutting and sighing noises.

Bambang felt panicky. Would it be better to leave now? There was still time to run. He started looking for the exit.

But he was stopped by the lights going down. There was a fanfare, and the following announcement was made: "We are honored to have the governor of our great city and his family attending our concert tonight. Please show your appreciation for all they do."

Everybody clapped, and a spotlight shone on a group of people in a box of extra-special velvet-and-gold seats off to one side. Bambang, who couldn't clap, looked up and saw something so surprising that he forgot about finding the exit.

Standing next to the governor,
looking much less grubby but rather
sulky, was George-from-the-Tree-in-the-
Park! Bambang waved his snout to say
hello. George caught sight of him, stopped
looking sulky, and waved back. He
lifted up a bag of caramels and winked.

The concert began. They sat
through a rather loud trumpet,
a rather quiet harp, a very
screechy violin, and a boy
who played the harmonica
with his nose. Then it was
Mango's turn. Bambang
held his breath as she
came out onstage.
She looked
smaller than
usual on
her own
under
the
lights.

"I am going to play 'City Nights.'"
Mango took a breath and lifted her
clarinet to her lips.

Then she let her breath out and
lowered her clarinet.

"I *am* going to play 'City Nights,'" she
said again. "But I'd much rather not play
it on my own. I have a very special friend
in the audience. Last night he showed
me what music can be. I play better
when he's with me. Bambang — won't
you come up?" Mango shielded her eyes
from the glare of the lights and looked
out over the rows of heads.

Bambang froze. He didn't know
what to do. Could he get on a stage?

Could he face all those people? He'd
never done anything like it before.
But then he'd never done anything
much except run and hide before he'd
met Mango. How many of the world's
wonders he had missed that way!

He could do anything with Mango.
He would do anything for Mango.
She'd asked because she needed him.
Trembling but determined, he rose from
his seat, walked down the aisle, and

climbed up onto the stage. He looked up
at Mango, and she smiled down at him.

Bambang knew he was safe. He'd
found his home.

Mango put her clarinet to her lips
once more—and then lowered it *again*.

"In case anyone isn't perfectly
clear, Bambang is a tapir. Not a pig
or a panda or a badger or a horse or
a skunk or a rhino. A tapir. *And* my
best friend."

Then she put her clarinet to her lips and kept it there, and they played and sang together just as they had on the bridge.

And when they finished, the audience found their hankies and wiped their eyes and blew their noses and clapped and clapped and clapped, while Mango and Bambang bowed and bowed and bowed.

"HURRAH!"

"BRAVO!"

And every single person in that
audience now knew what a tapir was.
Just like you do.